THE MYSTERIOUS VISITOR
STORIES OF THE PROPHET ELIJAH

BY NINA JAFFE

ILLUSTRATED BY ELIVIA SAVADIER

SCHOLASTIC PRESS ❧ NEW YORK

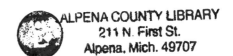

ACKNOWLEDGMENTS

The author is grateful to Yale University Press for permission to reprint and adapt "Hymn for Havdalah" which appears in *The Folk Literature of the Kurdistani Jews* by Yona Sabar (New Haven: Yale University Press, 1982).

In researching material for this book, the author gratefully acknowledges the library staff of the Jewish Theological Seminary and Hebrew Union College in New York City. Beatrice Silverman Weinreich, Senior Research Associate in Yiddish Folklore of the YIVO Institute for Jewish Research in New York City, and Professor Bezalel Narkiss, Nicholas Landau Professor of Art History at the Hebrew University in Jerusalem, provided invaluable background on the role of Elijah in Jewish folklore and history. Many thanks are also due to Cantor Gordon Piltch of the Conservative Synagogue Adath Israel of Riverdale and Aubrey Glazer, rabbinical student and filmmaker, for reviewing the text in regard to details of Jewish ritual and historical accuracy. To Professor Dov Noy, founder of the Israel Folktale Archives at Haifa University, Israel, and to Peninnah Schram, Director of the Jewish Storytelling Center, my deepest thanks for the scholarship and vision that help us keep the stories alive, the chain unbroken.

LIBRARY OF CONGRESS CATALOGING-IN-PUBLICATION DATA

JAFFE, NINA.
THE MYSTERIOUS VISITOR: STORIES OF THE PROPHET ELIJAH / NINA JAFFE;
ILLUSTRATED BY ELIVIA SAVADIER.
P. CM.
INCLUDES BIBLIOGRAPHICAL REFERENCES.
ISBN 0-590-48422-2
1. ELIJAH (BIBLICAL PROPHET)—LEGENDS. 2. ELIJAH (BIBLICAL PROPHET)—JUVENILE LITERATURE.
I. SAVADIER, ELIVIA, ILL. II. TITLE.
BS580.E4J34 1997
222'.5092—DC20   CIP   AC

12 11 10 9 8 7 6 5 4 3 2 1   7 8 9/9 0 1 2/0
PRINTED IN SINGAPORE
FIRST PRINTING, MARCH 1997

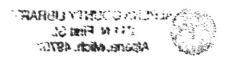

*For the Cohens—my dearest Uncle Manny and
Aunt Sylvia—with love always.*
—N.J.

*For Nancy Mellon—
Thank you for helping me unfold the fascinating archetypes
in these tales, and for your support.*
—Elivia

CONTENTS

HYMN FOR HAVDALAH

Elijah owns twelve caves.

He travels to the four corners of the world.

Elijah says, "I am Elijah.

"I stand behind the divine throne."

Elijah dwells among the angels.

He soars over the entire world in four orbits.

He brings us calm and good tidings.

Elijah works wonders.

Every night he travels to villages and towns.

He brings healing from all ailments.

Elijah performs many miracles.

When we make a request of him,

He grants blessings to every house in Israel.

— from *The Folk Literature of Kurdistani Jews*

INTRODUCTION

Elijah the Prophet is one of the most well-known of all characters in Jewish folklore. Many children in Jewish homes know him as the mysterious visitor who is invited every Passover to the Seder meal. Toward the end of the holiday ritual, the family members sing a song to Elijah and leave a goblet of wine for him at the table. When I was a child, I would run to open the door for Elijah. Whenever I came back to the table, his wineglass, which had been full before, was always half empty. Somehow, Elijah had come!

Elijah is important to Passover, but he is also a part of many other Jewish traditions, rituals, and stories. The reasons for this go far back into Jewish history. The story of Elijah first appears in the Bible in the Book of Kings I and II.

There he is portrayed as a strict prophet, who punishes King Ahab and his queen, Jezebel, for bringing false prophets and idol worshippers into the land of Israel. In the biblical story, Elijah also performs miracles. He visits a widow and although she has no food, he is able to make a small bit of meat and a tiny lamp of oil last for many days. Through prayers, he restores the breath of life back to her child. In the Bible, Elijah is sent by God to wander the desert and perform many difficult tasks. Finally, he is brought to the mountain of Carmel. There, Elisha, his traveling companion and disciple, sees Elijah carried up to heaven in a chariot of fire.

The idea that Elijah was a miracle worker and a healer was very popular in ancient times. Scenes depicting the miracles of Elijah have been found at the sites of synagogues built during the time of the Roman Empire. Scholars believe that many people traveled far distances to visit these sites, to seek healing and blessings. In 72 C.E. the Roman army destroyed the Temple in Jerusalem, and the Jewish people were dispersed all over the world. Some managed to stay in Israel, but most Jewish people migrated to other parts of the Middle East; to North Africa, India, and Spain; and to Eastern, Central, and Western Europe. Wherever they went, they brought with them their traditions, literature, laws, and beliefs, including stories about Elijah.

Slowly over time, as these stories were passed from one generation to the next, the image of Elijah changed from the strict, zealous prophet of the Bible. In the folk imagination, Elijah became the comforter, the healer, and the maker of miracles. Because it was written in the Torah that Elijah never died, Elijah was believed to be a messenger from heaven to earth. In story after story, he appears as a wanderer, a traveler who often comes to the aid of the poor, needy, and downtrodden. In the Jewish tradition, Elijah is also the one who will announce the coming of the Messiah and the redemption of the world.

At various times throughout the years of the dispersion of the Jewish people (called the Diaspora), Jews often suffered persecution in the new lands to which they had come. Elijah began to appear in many stories as a helper and a savior of the Jewish community. In other tales, he appears as a magician, a matchmaker, even a doctor!

During earlier centuries, when rabbinical sages struggled to study and practice the Torah in Israel and other parts of the ancient world, Elijah was also cast in the role of teacher and moral guide. In one such tale, a rabbi is walking down the road with Elijah. As they're walking, they see the remains of a dead animal, and the rabbi holds his nose. A little while later, they pass by a proud and haughty man, and this time Elijah holds *his* nose!

One book alone cannot possibly contain all the stories about Elijah. Today in Israel, the University of Haifa houses the Israel Folktale Archives, founded by the renowned folklore scholar, Dov Noy. These are the stories that Jewish immigrants from all over the world brought with them to the modern state of Israel. The archives contain thousands of Jewish folktales from cultures as diverse as Poland, Kurdistan, India, Morocco, and Ethiopia. Several hundred of these are stories that focus on or contain references to the Prophet Elijah.

For this book, I have chosen eight stories that are special to me. I hope they will lead you to discover more of these wonderful tales—to read, to share, and to tell—so that the blessings of Elijah, and his message of peace, will be with us for many generations to come.

THE DREAM

Long ago in Zabledov, there was a *melamed*, a Hebrew schoolteacher named Reb Yakov. He lived in a small hut on the top of a hill, near to the town's synagogue. He was very, very poor. In fact, the only possession he had worth anything at all was the big iron stove that sat in the middle of his tiny house. As long as he had enough wood, that stove kept him warm through all the storms and frosts of winter.

Every day, Reb Yakov would take his walking stick and go from house to house, giving lessons in return for a few coins, a bit of food, or clothing. He would teach the children the letters of the *alef–bet* and how to read the Torah and Talmud. But most of all, the children loved to gather around and hear him tell stories about the Prophet Elijah.

"Remember, children," Reb Yakov would say, "the Torah tells us that Elijah never died, but went straight up to heaven in a chariot of fire. He still comes to earth to help those in need, but he is hard to recognize! Sometimes he is disguised as a peasant, and sometimes as a nobleman. He can appear as a cobbler, a merchant, a peddler, or a soldier. So remember, be kind and gentle to anyone you meet, for you never know who you may be talking to!"

Years passed. One winter it was colder than it had ever

been before. Day after day, storms raged around the town of Zabledov. Blizzards blew and the snow came down to form in great drifts. Reb Yakov was an old man now, and even with his walking stick, it was hard for him to go from house to house. Little by little his small savings were used up, until one day Reb Yakov realized that he had nothing left. There was no more food in the house and not even a bit of kindling to put in his stove. That night, he put his head down on his hard, wooden bed. He was colder and hungrier than he had ever been before. "Who knows what tomorrow will bring?" he murmured to himself, as he huddled beneath the flimsy blankets that barely covered him.

Reb Yakov closed his eyes. As he fell asleep, he began to dream. In his dream, the wind whistled through the cracks in the walls and blew open the door of his house. A strange figure walked inside. He was tall and imposing, yet there was something familiar in his bearing. He had a long white beard and shining robes. It was the Prophet Elijah! And Elijah said to him, "Reb Yakov…Reb Yakov of Zabledov. Go to Warsaw. Stand by the eastern gates of the city, and you will hear the words meant only for you!"

In the chill light of morning, Reb Yakov rubbed his eyes. He remembered his dream, but he could not believe what he had seen and heard.

"After all," he said to himself, "I am an old man now, and Warsaw is miles away — even farther than Bialystok! How could I ever get there in this cold and snow? I'd better stay home."

That night, he laid his head down on his bed, still cold

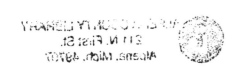

and hungry. But no sooner had he closed his eyes to sleep, when again he dreamed that the wind blew open the door of his house, and again, the Prophet Elijah stood before him. The prophet pointed his hand and said: "Reb Yakov—*go* to the city of Warsaw. Stand by the eastern gates, and you will hear the words meant only for you."

In the morning, Reb Yakov woke up and shook his head. "It is too far!" he said to himself. "It is too far to go only for a dream." But that very night, the third night in a row, he had the same dream. And the next morning, he wrapped his tattered cloak tightly around him, picked up his walking stick, and set off for Warsaw.

Down the hill he went, and out beyond the narrow streets of Zabledov. He walked for many days, struggling across icy rivers and snowbound valleys, through mountain passes and down muddy roads, until he reached the city of Warsaw.

When Reb Yakov arrived, he stood by the eastern gate. All day long he waited. Many people passed by on their way in and out of the city, but no one said a word to him. The sun began to set, and as the last golden rays flickered across the sky, Reb Yakov leaned heavily against a tall iron street-lamp, his head sunk on to his chest. He had nowhere to sleep, no food to eat, and Zabledov was miles away.

"I should just find a corner somewhere," he said to himself, "where I will go and wait for the end of my life to come."

Suddenly, he heard someone speak to him. It was the officer of the eastern gate, a Polish soldier, who waved and said, "You there, old man! You've been standing there all day long, looking as if you were waiting for someone, but no one has come. You have traveled far, I can tell. Come, I will give you some food and drink, but you must promise to tell me why an old one like you has come all this way to Warsaw!"

Reb Yakov followed the soldier to his guardhouse. Inside, a small hearth fire burned in the corner. It warmed him to the bone, after his long journey through the snow and ice. The soldier gave him a plate of black bread with cheese, and a bowl of hot soup. Reb Yakov ate till his hunger was satisfied. When Reb Yakov could speak again, the soldier said to him, "Now tell me, my friend. My days are long and monotonous. I hardly ever hear news from outside Warsaw. Why have you come all the way here?"

And Reb Yakov began, "Well, you see, sir, this has been a cold, hard winter. With all the snow and blizzards, I haven't always known where my next meal would come from. Then one night, a few days ago, I had a dream…"

"A dream?" The soldier laughed and slapped his boots. "Do you mean to tell me you have come all this way because of a *dream*?"

Reb Yakov could only nod his head. He was about to go on when the soldier interrupted him. "I should have known by the looks of you that you were one to believe in dreams. Why, just look at the rags on your back and the holes in your shoes!" He laughed again till his sides shook.

Reb Yakov stood up. "Thank you, my friend, for sharing your meal and warm fire, but now, it is time for me to go."

He picked up his walking stick and started out the door. As he stepped outside, the soldier stopped laughing long enough to catch his breath. He called to Reb Yakov one last time.

"Wait, you've told me your story. It's only fair that I tell you one in return. You're not the only one to have dreams, you know. Why, just a few days ago, I too had a dream. Yes, that's right. I dreamed that an old man with a long white beard came into my house. He told me that if I were to go to some Godforsaken little town, I think it was called Zabledov, that's right. If I were to go to Zabledov and look for the house of a certain Reb Yakov who lives in a little hut on top of a hill, I would find underneath his iron stove — a treasure! But who needs a dream treasure? I like the sound of my own coins, right here in my pocket! That's all the treasure I need! Good-bye then, and a good journey to you — and your dreams!"

Reb Yakov lifted his hat. "Thank you, my friend, for all you have shared with me."

Then he began to walk as fast as he could the long way back to Zabledov. Down the muddy roads he traveled, across the valleys and rivers and through the snowdrifts. Finally, he saw his town in the distance. Through the narrow streets he walked, up the hill, past the synagogue. When he reached his house, he took his walking stick and used it to pry apart the wooden boards near the stove. With all his strength, he pushed and he pulled at each piece of wood. And there, under his great iron stove, he struck something hard. It was a wooden box covered with dust and ashes. Slowly, with trembling hands, he opened the lid of the box. Inside, he saw that the box was filled with a sparkling treasure—gold coins, diamonds, and rubies, worth enough to feed him for many winters to come.

From that day, Reb Yakov never again had to walk from house to house to see his students. Instead, he had a beautiful *cheder* built on the top of the hill, right next to his own home. The cheder was filled with books and scrolls, open to any visitor who wished to learn. Every day, the children of Zabledov would go there to study the letters of the alef–bet, and to learn how to read the Torah and the Talmud.

But most of all, in winter, summer, autumn, or spring, the children loved to gather around Reb Yakov and hear him tell stories of the Prophet Elijah!

2
ELIJAH IN THE
MARKETPLACE

Once in Egypt, near the city of Alexandria, there lived a farmer named Nathan. Generations before, when the Holy Temple in Jerusalem had been destroyed by the Romans, his ancestors had picked up their belongings and traveled overland to Egypt. There they found land, and began to till the soil as their family had always done. The land was passed on from father to son, and now Nathan, with his wife and children, was the one to wake up before dawn and see to his fields. He tended his olive trees with care and always planted and harvested

his grains in time with the seasons. He lived in a small house made of clay bricks with a straw-covered roof. While Nathan tended the fields, his wife, Johanna, worked in the garden or wove cloth from the cotton they grew to sell in the nearby marketplace. His children, Ilana and Tovah, worked, too. Sometimes they would go to the well to bring water to their father when the Mediterranean sun grew high in the sky and the ground scorched his feet. Sometimes they sat in the shade of the garden and helped their mother choose the sweetest pomegranates and the finest dates they had picked from their nearby grove.

Every week, Nathan would pile his wagon high with his grains and goods, harness his two oxen, and set off for the marketplace of Alexandria. And as he rode, he would sing to himself a favorite counting song from his childhood, a song from the Passover Seder. *"Echad Mi Yodea*? Who knows one? I know one! One is our God who is on heaven and on earth." And so, singing and whisking the flies from his oxen's backs, he would make his way to the market.

One year, the *hamsin*, the hot winds from the Sahara Desert, blew more ferociously than ever before. The river Nile had barely flooded her banks, and the winter rains had not come at all. There was a terrible drought in the land. It was near to Passover, and for Nathan and his family there was barely enough wheat in the fields to make their *matzah*, much less bring it to sell in the marketplace. One morning, before the heat of the sun began to rise, Nathan woke up and walked out into his parched fields.

"Oh, Lord," he said, "how can I feed my family? How will

we sit together and celebrate the Passover, when we can barely move from hunger and thirst, and my fields are withering before my eyes?"

Just then, he saw walking toward him a *fellah*, an Egyptian peasant, with a *kaffiyeh* cloth wrapped around his head. "*Salaam Aley-kum*," the peasant greeted him.

"*Aley-kum Salaam*," repeated Nathan, as was the custom.

"I've seen your fields and your cattle," said the fellah. "Your family must be suffering greatly. But I know a way to help you."

Nathan was surprised to hear a stranger speaking to him this way. But he was curious to hear more. "That is kind of you, neighbor," he said, "but how can you help?"

"I know that today is market day. Take me to the market, and once we're there you can sell me as a slave. Then you can use the money from the sale to find what you need for your family."

Nathan shook his head. "That is kind of you, but I have never sold anyone as a slave, and I don't intend to start now. We will manage to get along somehow."

As they spoke, the sun's rays began to reach across the morning sky. In a sudden instant, the peasant's kaffiyeh dropped to the ground. A crown of glowing light surrounded his head. Nathan blinked his eyes. Was the sunlight playing tricks on him?

The peasant's simple cotton wrap fell away, too. He stood in the fields, tall and serene, dressed in silvery robes. "Nathan, it is I, Elijah the Prophet. The Holy One has heard your prayers and I have come to answer them. Take me to the

their hooves echoing on the dusty cobbled streets.

Nathan shook his head. Could this all have been a dream? But no, for there at his feet were the three bags of coins. Eighty thousand dinars! That was enough to keep his family clothed and fed for years to come! Thanking God in his prayers, he set about to fill his wagon with grains and wheat, and then he set off for home.

Johanna and the children greeted him joyfully on his return. "Father, father! Now we can prepare the Passover meal!" they cried.

Meanwhile, Elijah rode on with the sultan. When they reached the palace, the sultan ordered him to be fed in the royal kitchen. Then he commanded his new slave to appear before him. "Now that you are here, show me what you can do! What are your skills?"

"Your highness," said the noble slave who stood before him, "I have traveled over many parts of the earth and have learned many things. In Arabia, I learned to play a magic flute." Out of his pocket he pulled a silver flute and began to play. His melody was so sweet that all the birds in the palace gardens stopped their singing and flew to the window to listen to his song.

"A song is nice, but what else can you do?"

"In the streets of Baghdad, I learned to juggle a hundred crystal balls."

"Have my servants bring one hundred crystal balls to the palace!" said the sultan. Elijah waited. The servants ran out, and soon they came back bearing one hundred crystal balls neatly ordered on ten silver trays. Then, one by one, Elijah threw them up in the air. He was so skillful that he kept them all moving in circles and graceful figure eights. The crystal balls danced in the air. Not one did he drop. Everyone in the palace watched in awe.

"Oh, that is all very well," said the sultan, "but those are magic tricks you can learn anywhere. What I need is something more than tricks and music. I need something that will stand forever, that people will remember me by for generations to come! Now you are a slave, but I can give you your freedom, on one condition. I rule over towns and cities across the land, but outside my window is a field of dry grass and dusty soil. I need a new palace. And this palace can be like no other one in the world. Its walls must be of gold and its floors of sparkling gems. The gardens must be full of flowers that bloom in all seasons, and the threshold of every doorway must be carved of ebony and cedar wood. Make this palace for me and if by six months the work is complete, I will set you free."

Elijah nodded. "I will complete your wishes, your highness, but I, too, have a condition."

"And what might that be?" asked the sultan.

"If I build the palace as you desire, then you must not only give me my freedom, but all the slaves in your kingdom must go free as well."

"Very well," said the sultan. "It shall be as you say." But of course, he never believed for a moment that this palace could be built. He was sure that he would be able to keep all of his slaves forever.

Elijah nodded again and stepped away from the sultan's throne.

That night, as everyone in the palace slept, Elijah went to

the window, and there he prayed. "Oh, Lord, you sent me here to help Nathan, the farmer who has always kept his faith to you. Hear now my prayers. Help me to do the work for the sultan, so that all obligations will be fulfilled in time for the first night of Passover, the Feast of Freedom."

That night, all in the palace were asleep. But if they had looked out into the distance, they would have seen a strange and wondrous sight. The stars shone from above as always. But on this night hundreds of twinkling lights seemed to come down to earth as well, hovering over the fields, while a thousand silvery voices filled the night air. "Put it up here! No, set it down there. That's what the sultan's plan said!"

At dawn, the sultan arose from his bed. After dressing in his royal garments, he walked over to the window and looked out across his lands, as he did every morning. The empty acres of grass and windswept soil of the day before had vanished. Instead, there stood the palace of his dreams. Its walls were of gold; its towers shone in the sun. He could see gardens full of flowers and doorways carved in ebony and cedar, just as he had planned.

The sultan ran to look for the slave he had purchased in the marketplace the day before. He searched for him in every corner of the palace. He sent his soldiers out to comb the surrounding countryside, but they returned, shaking their heads. All the sultan could find of him was the silver flute, lying near the fountain in the royal courtyard. "This was no slave, but an angel sent from heaven," he murmured. Humbled and bowed with awe, he sent out a command that very day that all the slaves in his kingdom were to be freed as he had promised. And he called the palace "Home of the Angels," so his people would remember the miraculous event from that day forward.

Inside his own clay brick home, Nathan and his family prepared for the Passover. Even in the drought, they now had enough of what they needed to make *matzah* and sweet *charoset*. They prepared a lamb to roast and invited neighbors to share the Seder meal with them. Johanna wove a white cloth to spread over the table. Ilana prepared the Seder plate with charoset, salt water, and bitter herbs. And Tovah filled the special goblet of wine, the Cup of Elijah, which they saved all year for that night.

But Nathan was worried. Elijah, he knew, had been sold to the sultan.

What had become of him? Sadly, Nathan stepped outside his house and went into the fields. As he stood there, an Egyptian peasant, a fellah, his head wrapped in a kaffiyeh, stopped to greet him.

"Salaam Aley-kum," he said.

"Aley-kum Salaam," Nathan replied.

"So—on this night you will celebrate the Passover," the peasant said.

"That is so," said Nathan.

"Then all is as it should be," said the peasant, "and I can be on my way."

He picked up his staff and waved to Nathan as he set off down the road.

It was only when he had completely disappeared from sight that Nathan returned to his home, ready to sing the holiday prayers with a full and peaceful heart.

3
THE THREE BROTHERS

Long ago in France, there was a small town that stood in a valley near the flowing waters of the river Loire. The town was surrounded by walls to protect the people from attack during times of war. Many of the noblemen of the town had left to fight in the Crusades. But still, the peasants and the farmers, the merchants and the craftsmen kept to their work and trades.

Now in this town there lived a man named Joseph. He was a merchant of silks and spices, who often traveled far from home to trade and sell clothes and precious garments from the East. Joseph was happy, for although he traveled far, he knew that whenever he returned home, there to greet him would be his lovely wife, Rebecca—and their three sons, Benjamin, Saul, and Jacob. While he was away, Rebecca cared for the children. She made sure that they studied Hebrew. She engaged a tutor, who would sit with them during the week and teach them how to read and understand the Torah and *halacha*, the ways of Jewish law and tradition.

While they studied, Rebecca would tend to the spice garden by the side of the house. There she would plant and carefully water the fragrant herbs of mint, basil, and thyme. The flowers would always bloom in their season, and a gently hanging willow tree gave the shade that the garden needed for protection against the summer sun. Whenever Joseph returned home from his travels, his wife and children ran to greet him joyfully. And if it was just before Sabbath when he stepped in the door, they would all sit together by the open window of their house and breathe in the lovely scents from the garden. As the sun began to set, Rebecca would light the candles, and they would recite the blessings over the wine and the fresh *challah* bread. When Sabbath was ended, the children would run outside and look up at the night sky. As soon as the first three stars appeared, they would run into the house again. Rebecca would pass around the spice box, for the sweetest of spices she saved for *Havdalah*, the candle-lighting ceremony at the end of the Sabbath. They would breathe in the aroma of the spices, and each son would have a turn dipping the braided candle into the plate of wine to put out its flame.

As they bid farewell to the Sabbath, they would sing the special Havdalah prayer, *"Eliyahu ha navi, Eliyahu ha Tishbi, Eliyahu, Eliyahu, Eliyahu ha Giladi.* Elijah the Prophet, Elijah the Tishbite, Elijah of Gilead, may the days of the Messiah come speedily."

One year, Joseph had to be away longer than usual on his spring journey. While he was away, a terrible plague passed through the town. Men, women, or children, the plague spared no one. Many became ill. Some died. When Joseph heard the news, he traveled home as fast as he could, but by the time he arrived it was too late. All his children had been spared, but Rebecca lay dying. "Remember, my children and my husband," she whispered, "you will always have the spice garden. Care for it and tend it well."

And so, Joseph's days of traveling were over. Now he stayed at home to raise his sons and watch over their learning and studies. Benjamin, Saul, and Jacob grew to be fine young men. Each learned a trade, and Joseph was proud of them. When he reached old age and knew that his days, too, were numbered, he called his children to him and said, "My sons, I give you my blessings. My inheritance will be divided equally among you. You must only promise one thing. As long as you live within the walls of this home, I ask you to care for your mother's spice garden, for it was her precious gift to you."

The three sons promised. After Joseph died, they buried him in the town cemetery. Benjamin said, "Father wished for us to watch over the spice garden. These days there are many thieves and vandals abroad, and who knows but they may wish to pillage our home, now that our revered father is no longer here."

"You're right," said Saul. "Soon we must leave this house to practice our trades. But while we are here, let us care for it well."

"Perhaps we should sleep in the garden to guard it from any misfortune," said Jacob. "Since the inheritance is divided equally among us, let us also divide our responsibilities for the watch."

So the three sons agreed that each night one of them would sleep in the garden.

On the first night of their watch, Benjamin, the eldest, spread a woolen blanket under the willow tree. Although he tried to stay awake, the soft breezes and chirping of crickets lulled him into a nodding doze and soon he was fast asleep. Just as the moon rose into the sky, he felt someone tap him gently on the shoulder. He shook himself awake, and there before him stood a man with a long pilgrim's cloak and staff. "Excuse me, young sir, but I am a pilgrim on my way to Jerusalem, the Holy City. May I rest awhile in your garden?"

At first Benjamin was afraid, but he saw that the man's face was kindly, so he offered him a place by the roots of a willow tree. "Here, my friend," he said, "this spice garden was a gift to our family from our dear mother, who has long ago passed way. Tonight is my turn to guard over it, but you may rest awhile beneath this tree."

So the pilgrim set down his staff, wrapped himself in his cloak, whispered a short prayer, and seemed to fall into a deep sleep.

Just before dawn, Benjamin awoke with a start. The pilgrim was standing over him, a smile on his face. "Benjamin, you were kind to me during the night and gave me rest and comfort. I have come here with a message for you. Because of your kindness and the good deeds of your parents before you, I can grant you a wish. Soon you will leave this house to go out on your own into the world. One of three things may come to you with this wish. You may acquire wealth, you may acquire great wisdom, or you may find a wise and righteous wife. Which one do you choose?"

Benjamin did not have to think long. "Stranger, I thank you kindly for you words, and if it is true that one of these wishes shall be mine, then I wish to be one who will acquire great wealth, so that my family shall never know hunger or want."

34

Instantly, the pilgrim disappeared. But lying at Benjamin's feet was a small sack, and at the bottom of the sack was a single silver coin. Now Benjamin left the garden and walked down the road. He thought he would buy some bread for his morning meal. He came to the baker's shop and asked for a loaf of bread. When he reached into the bag, there were not one but ten coins, enough to pay for the bread and a jug of cider besides. Wherever he went, the coins always renewed themselves.

So Benjamin left home to see where his good fortune would take him. Soon he became a wealthy man, living in a fine house surrounded by fields, with his own servants and peasants to work the land.

The next night, it was Saul's turn to sleep in the garden. He, too, wrapped himself in a woolen blanket and lay asleep under the stars of the night sky. When the moon had risen, the pilgrim once again appeared with his staff in hand and asked for a place to rest. Saul, in his mother's name, invited him to take a spot by the willow tree. Before the light of dawn began to fill the sky, Saul felt a tapping on his shoulder. It was the pilgrim, offering him the three wishes. And Saul, who had always loved to read and study, immediately said, "If any of these wishes can come to me, then let me have great knowledge and wisdom, for it is said that Torah is the greatest wealth of all, and I wish to be a great scholar."

The pilgrim reached in his traveling bag and gave him many books of knowledge—the Torah, the Talmud, and other holy books. Saul opened the first book to read, but no sooner had he touched it than he knew and understood all of its contents, and he found he could speak with wisdom and authority on each of the books that he opened. So Saul left home and went off to become a great and learned man.

On the third night, it was Jacob's turn to sleep in the garden. Now Jacob, being the youngest, was sad that his brothers had departed. He, too, wished for adventure and good fortune. But he knew that he must keep his promise and stay the night in their mother's garden. Although he was the youngest, he always remembered his mother, her kind face, her sweet words, and her face as she lit the candles and sang the blessings for the Sabbath. The garden had been a special place for him, and he wished to guard it well.

As evening fell, he wrapped himself in the blanket, bundling up against the cool night breeze, and fell asleep under the night sky. Toward midnight, he felt a tapping on his shoulder. It was the pilgrim, asking for a place of rest. "Pilgrim," said Jacob, "I can see you have traveled from afar, and your journey to Jerusalem is longer still. You must have great adventures to relate and stories to tell, but for now you need sleep." So he moved over and gave his spot to the traveler. Then he fell fast asleep.

Before dawn, someone awoke him with a gentle tap. "Young man," the pilgrim said, "because of your kindness and the good deeds of your parents, three wishes may be granted to you." As soon as he heard them, Jacob knew what he wanted, "My father was blessed with a wise and righteous wife," he said, "and if I can have a hand in my own destiny, then that is all I could wish for."

The pilgrim smiled. "The other wishes I could grant by

reaching into my own pocket or the sack on my back. But for your wish, you, too, must become a traveler and a pilgrim."

Jacob shook off the last of sleep and set off down the road with the pilgrim beside him. They walked for some time, till they came to an inn. Jacob was tired and weary. He was looking forward to a night in the inn, but the pilgrim led him, instead, to the barn. Once inside, the pilgrim said to his companion, "We will sleep here tonight, and in the morning we will go inside and you can ask for the hand of the innkeeper's daughter."

But while Jacob slept, the pilgrim listened to the ducks and the geese talking and quacking to each other. "I hope that young man is not looking for his bride here," they said to each other, "for the people in this house are wicked and cruel!" The pilgrim understood the language of the animals. He knew they could not stay at the inn any longer.

The next morning, they got up and traveled down the road until they came to another inn. Again they entered the barn and the pilgrim said, "This innkeeper, too, has a daughter, and tomorrow you will ask for her hand." So Jacob slept, but the pilgrim listened to the ducks and the geese. "Oh, I hope the young man doesn't find his bride here," they said, "for the master and his family are wicked and hard-hearted!"

And the pilgrim knew they had to move on. The next morning, they left the inn and traveled down the road till they came to a poor country tavern. Again they slept in the barn. The pilgrim listened carefully to the animals. "Oh," said the sheep, "that young man is lucky indeed if he is to marry the tavernkeeper's daughter. She is kind to us and feeds us every day!"

Now the tavernkeeper's daughter was truly kind and generous, as the farm creatures had said. Her name was Leah. As soon as Jacob saw her, he knew that he wished her to be his wife. Although he was alone and without family, the pilgrim spoke well of him and the parents of the girl agreed to the match. When they stood under the wedding canopy, the bride's father stood with her and the pilgrim stood with Jacob.

After the wedding, the pilgrim turned to Jacob. "I have fulfilled my mission," he said. "I must go on my journey to the Holy City. Now take your wife and make a home together, and may all go well with you."

Years passed. Wars came and went. Princes were crowned and ships traveled the great oceans. But life went on for the three sons of Joseph and Rebecca. One day, as Benjamin sat in the grand hall of his home, he heard a knock on his door. He waved to a servant. "Go see who is there!" At his behest, the servant opened the door, and there stood a traveler, covered with dust, holding a staff in his hand. "I have come to see the master of this house. Long ago, he did me a kindness, and I wish to thank him."

But when Benjamin came to the door, he only looked at the traveler and scoffed. "What's a beggar like you doing knocking at the front door of my house! Go to the back, and maybe there will be some scraps for you!" And he commanded the servant to slam the door shut. The pilgrim walked on.

After going down many a road and twisted path, he came to the house of Saul. Saul's study was as large as a banquet hall. Shelves of books reached to the ceiling, and all day long he sat and studied, pondering the meaning of each and every word. The traveler knocked on the door.

"May I come in?" he asked. "I have heard of your great wisdom and knowledge. I, too, have studied the great books, and I would like to talk over some questions in these texts with you."

Saul, shifting the spectacles from his nose, looked at the traveler. "Now, what makes you think that a dirty, dusty wanderer like you would have anything of value to say to me? I already know everything there is to know from the holy books, and I certainly don't want to waste my time talking things over with a vagabond like you!"

And Saul led him to the door and showed him the way out without even waiting to hear his reply.

The traveler walked on, until he came to the Loire valley. Nestled in a town by the river, there was a house that he remembered well, for it was surrounded by a lovely spice garden whose fragrance filled the air as he approached. When he knocked at the door, a woman opened it. Seeing his dusty clothes and ragged shoes, she did not even wait for his request but invited him into the house. There, she bathed his feet and gave him a meal. Only after he had rested and eaten did she ask him, "Sir, you have traveled from afar. Wherever fate has taken you, we are glad to welcome you to our house. My husband, Jacob, will return home soon, and I'm sure he will want to know how we can assist you on your travels."

The traveler began to speak, but just at that moment Jacob himself entered the house. His hair was gray and his dress was simple, but he smiled when he saw the traveler.

"Welcome, my friend, it has been many years since we have met. Your journey, I know, has been a long one. As you see, we have stayed here in my parents' house. Our fortune is not great, but we are happy and content."

The pilgrim held out his hand to Jacob and Leah. "My friends," he said, "many years ago, I was sent to grant the three children of Joseph and Rebecca three wishes. Your brothers have made their wishes, but neither of them has profited by wealth or knowledge. Instead, Benjamin's wealth has only made him cruel and selfish, and Saul's knowledge has made him proud and arrogant. Your brothers did not know how to use their gifts. I give them now to you and Leah, their rightful owners, for you two together will know how to use these gifts wisely and well."

And with that, the pilgrim snapped his fingers. In his right hand, a bag with silver coins appeared, and he handed it to Jacob. He snapped his fingers again, and this time a sack filled with holy books appeared, and this he handed to Leah. "Keep them and use them. In time, your brothers will return, and you will teach them the lessons they could not learn by themselves. For you, Jacob, chose a good companion. You have lived together in peace and honor, and so your parents' wishes are fulfilled. You have tended the spice garden well, the gardens of your hearts."

As the pilgrim disappeared, a faint yet familiar melody filled the air. It was the melody of Havdalah, the melody Jacob's mother and father sang with them every week, and Jacob smiled, for at last he knew who the pilgrim was. The sun began to set, and as Jacob and Leah looked out the window, they saw two lone figures making their way up the path. Three stars rose in the sky as the brothers followed the path—past the willow tree, past the fragrance of basil and thyme, toward the lights waiting inside, toward home.

4
ELIJAH AND
THE FISHER BOY

One day, Elijah the Prophet was walking down the road. It was a bright, sunny day. Trees branches blew softly in the wind, and small birds chirped around his head. As he walked, he began to think about all that he saw as he traveled in the world.

"There is so much unhappiness," he said to himself. "People are always getting into trouble of one kind or another. There is meanness, cruelty, and injustice of all kinds. At this rate, the Messiah will never come."

Elijah kept walking and thinking. "Some people have health and good fortune, while others suffer. Then they become jealous of each other, and the troubles begin. Humans need a little more kindness. A little more help all around. Then life on earth would change soon enough. People would learn to live in peace, and I could bring the Messiah at last."

Elijah went on his way, still thinking these thoughts. "I have to find one person, just one person to try my theory out on."

Just at that moment, Elijah tripped over something and almost fell over. "Watch where you're going, can't you?" a voice said.

Elijah looked down and saw before him a young fisherman. The boy was sitting on a wooden box next to a stream, holding his fishing rod over the water. Elijah had tripped on his line. The young fisherman sighed. He straightened out the line and cast his hook into the water again with a dejected look on his face.

"Greetings, young man," said Elijah. "Sorry I tripped on your line, but you look so sad and forlorn. What's the matter? The fish aren't biting today?"

"Hah!" said the young man, whose name was Yossel. "Day after day I sit and throw my hook into the water. If I'm lucky, I catch one fish a week to sell at the marketplace. It's not a great life, but I have to fish to help feed my family. Oh, if only I had another job. What wonderful things I could do in the world!"

Hmmm, Elijah thought. Maybe this is just the one I've been looking for!

"Well," said Elijah, "if that is indeed the case, then you're in luck. I can grant your wish. What would you like to do?"

"I've always wanted to be a baker. Then I could help the poor and feed the hungry, and be a happy man besides!"

Instantly, Yossel found himself in a baker's shop, wearing a clean white apron and a white cap on his head. "Happy at last!" he said.

Elijah went on his way. A few days later, he returned to see how the baker was doing. The young man's apron was crusty with dough and his cap was torn in two.

"This is a miserable job!" said the young man. "Every day I have to put my hands in the oven to bake bread. They're always getting burned, and I have to fill the orders, one right after the other, with no rest in between. This is no job for me!"

Elijah said, "Well, my son, you can have a better job. What do you wish?"

"Let me be a banker. I wouldn't have to get my hands dirty, and I could distribute money to the poor." So Elijah waved his hands and Yossel instantly was transformed. Now he was wearing a black suit with a tie, and cuff links on the sleeves of his silk shirt. "You're on your way to the bank!" Elijah said, and bid him farewell.

A few days later, Elijah went to pay Yossel a visit. "How are things going?" he asked.

Yossel groaned. "Do you call this proper work? Day after day I have to add and subtract, multiply and divide, count the money, and write up ledgers and columns without stopping. This is not the job for me!"

"Well, my son," said Elijah, "you can do better. What do you wish?"

"Let me be a judge. I could wear long robes, and everyone would respect my opinion. I could help make laws that are fair for everyone."

"Let it be so," said Elijah, and there stood Yossel before him, dressed in a long black robe with a white wig settled on his head. "You'll find this work interesting, I'm sure."

Elijah went off on a journey. When he returned, he went to find Yossel. There he was, in his courtroom, scratching his head and muttering to himself. As soon as he saw Elijah, he cheered up. "I'm glad you've come. This judgeship won't work for me at all. Cases pile up and every day I have to listen to lawyers arguing and plaintiffs complaining. A judge's life is no life for me!"

Elijah smiled patiently. "Then what would suit you better, my son?"

"I'd like to be a general and command a thousand troops. Then I would be happy."

Elijah waved his hands, and instantly Yossel was dressed in full military uniform, with medals and stripes covering his shoulders and a handsome steed tossing his head beside him.

"There you are," said Elijah. "Now you can do some good for the world." And he left Yossel in a peaceful state of mind, thinking how happy he would be.

In a few days, he came back to see how Yossel the general was doing. Yossel was pacing back and forth, stamping his feet with impatience. "This is no job for me!" he said. "Every day, the lieutenants need to hear my orders. I have to plan strategies and read a hundred maps. I have to make sure the troops are fed and that all the horses are in good condition. This is no way for me to live!"

Elijah sighed. "What do you wish, my son?"

"I'd like to be king. Then I could sit on my throne and rule the land with justice and wisdom, and no one would tell me what to do!"

"Then so shall it be." Elijah waved his hand, and instantly Yossel stood before him dressed in silks and the finest velvet, with a golden crown on his head and a hundred servants beside him.

Elijah smiled, "Now you'll be happy and do some good for the world!"

And he left Yossel to his throne. A few days later, he returned to see how the king was doing. He found Yossel in the throne room, absentmindedly picking at his royal cloak. "Well, my son, how is life as king of all the land?"

Yossel sighed. "Since you ask—it's miserable. I spend all day signing royal decrees and listening to my subjects tell me all their problems. Then it's time to stand up for hours at a time at royal celebrations. The life of a king is not an easy one, I can tell you that!"

Elijah stroked his beard. "Well, my son, what do you wish?"

And Yossel said, "I think it would really be best if I were God. That way, the whole world would go according to my plan and everything would be just as it should!"

Elijah knew that Yossel would never be satisfied. He waved his hand one last time, and as he did a crack of thunder burst through the sky. Instantly, Yossel found himself back on his box, his fishing rod in hand, his bait on the hook. The boy gazed around and then shrugged his shoulders. "I feel as though I've been somewhere faraway," he said to himself, "but I must have been dreaming." Just then, he felt something tug on the line.

"Maybe the fishing life isn't so bad, after all," Yossel said, as he pulled a trout, his first catch of the week, from the water's edge. He stood up, put the fish in his bucket, and walked home happily to his family.

Elijah picked up his stick and smiled to himself.

"Next time, I won't be so impatient. After all, God created the world and all its creatures just as they are. Human beings will have to find their own way to peace and happiness." And with these thoughts in his mind, he set off down the road, while the birds in their nests chirped to him softly in the light of the setting sun.

5

THE WOMAN WITH THE FACE OF A DONKEY

Once in Morocco there lived a great scholar. He was renowned for his knowledge and understanding of all the books of the Torah. When he would speak about the law, students from miles around would come to hear his words.

The scholar lived in a house outside of the city of Rabat. For many years, he and his wife lived there in happiness and contentment. The couple had six sons, each of them strong and healthy, but the scholar and his wife were sad, for they had no daughter to bless their home.

One day, as the scholar's wife was walking to visit a neighbor, she heard a strange noise by the roadside. She followed the sound and saw a farmer, sitting on his wagon. But the wagon wouldn't budge. It was stuck in the mud. The farmer was cracking the whip over the back of his donkey. The donkey pulled with all his might, but still the wagon wouldn't budge. The farmer cursed and beat the poor animal with even greater force.

The scholar's wife drew near and said, "Sir, why do you beat a poor animal? He, too, is one of God's creatures. Surely you can find a better way to move your cart."

The farmer turned his face to look at her, and she saw that his eyes were green. He stood up to speak, and she saw that even in the bright sunlight he cast no shadow on the ground.

"Meddler, why do you interfere? If you care about a donkey so much, then I say, let your next child be born to look like one!" And with a howl he cracked the whip one more time. The donkey lurched forward, gazing at the woman with a sorrowful face, and they trotted off down the road.

The scholar's wife continued on to her neighbors. She was troubled by what she had seen, but spoke not a word of it to her husband. Months later, there was great joy in the scholar's house. Another child was to be born! The midwife came every day to visit the mother-to-be, bringing her special herbs and teas to keep her healthy and strong until the time of the baby's birth.

Finally the day arrived. A newborn baby's wailing cry was heard from inside the house, and everyone rejoiced. The child was born. It was alive and healthy! But when the midwife stepped outside, there was a look of horror on her face. "Come inside," she whispered to the scholar. "You must see for your-self." Indeed, the seventh child had been born—the baby girl they had all been waiting for. But there could be no rejoicing in the house that day for, as everyone could see, the baby had been born with the face of a donkey.

In sorrow, the scholar's wife told her husband what had happened that day by the roadside, so long ago. "Ah, my dear wife," he said, "that must have been a *djinn*, a wandering spirit, you met by the roadside. Some are good, but some are evil. What can we do to lift this curse?"

The scholar sought advice from the greatest rabbis of

Morocco. They offered special prayers on his wife's behalf and gave the scholar amulets with powerful blessings to help reverse the curse. But nothing worked. The child was healthy in all ways. But the curse of the djinn remained.

The scholar and his wife loved their daughter. They knew they would care for her always, but to protect her from the world they raised her in a separate room, hidden behind a heavy curtain. Despite her animal face, the girl learned to speak, as other children did. Her father noticed, too, that she was bright and quick, and so he decided that he would raise her in the knowledge of Torah. The girl learned to read in Hebrew and Aramaic, the ancient languages of the Talmudic sages. As she grew older, she studied for hours at a time. Behind the heavy curtain that guarded her, she grew wise and learned.

Years passed, and one day a knock was heard at the scholar's door. He went to open it, and there before him stood a young man, tired and dusty from traveling. "I've come from afar, because I seek knowledge and understanding of the Torah and our sacred books. Your name is known far and wide. Please let me come and study with you."

The scholar smiled. "Of course you may come and study. The sages say that the world stands on three things: on study, prayer, and deeds of loving kindness, but study of Torah is equal to all three. My house is a house of learning and you are welcome here. But first, let us feed you and give you rest." So the young man stayed with the scholar. After they had eaten a full evening meal, the scholar took the young man to his study.

The room had walls painted white, adorned with intricate paper-cut scrolls of birds and flowers. Books and parchment lay everywhere. The young man noticed, though, that one corner of the room was covered from floor to ceiling with a heavy velvet curtain. He wondered about it, but he spoke not a word, for here he was a guest.

They began to study. First the rabbi would quote from a text and ask the young man a question. Then the young man would find an answer and prove he was right by point-ing to yet another quote. Back and forth they talked and read, pointed and argued. And always the scholar would lead the young man on, to look deeper and deeper into the meaning of the words. Always the young man could depend on himself to find an answer. But finally, the scholar asked him a question that no one had ever asked him before. The young man pondered over it for many minutes. He looked through all the books—those he had brought, and those that lay before him. Still, the answer would not come. Finally the scholar said, "I will leave you now to think this matter over. In the morning, we will discuss it again." And he left.

The young man continued to pore over books, to search for the answer, and still it would not come. Finally, in despair and exhaustion, he laid his head on the table to rest. As he lay there, half-asleep and half-awake, he heard a voice. It was the most beautiful voice he had ever heard—like a bell, or a shepherd's flute echoing through the moun-tain meadows. The voice seemed to come from inside the room. And it spoke words so wise and sweet that he lis-tened as if in a trance. The lilting voice gave him the answer he had been looking for, the answer to the most difficult of all questions that the scholar had put before him. Quickly, he wrote down the words he was hearing.

In the morning, when the scholar came to see him, the young man spoke to him quietly. "Here is the answer to your question. I studied for many hours but could not discover it. But during the night I heard a voice, like the voice of an angel from heaven. The voice came from somewhere in this room. Who gave me the answer? Was it human or spirit that spoke to me?"

The scholar smiled sadly. "You heard the voice of my daughter. That is who spoke with you during the night."

The young man stood up. "Then that is why I have been led here, for she is my destined bride and I will have no other."

The scholar shook his head. "No, my son, you do not know what you wish. My daughter cannot marry you. She is ill. She can never be your bride." But the young man stood his ground. He refused to budge and would accept neither food nor drink until the scholar and his wife promised their daughter to him in marriage. And in the end, they had to agree.

The day of the wedding arrived. In the scholar's garden, the family gathered as the bride and groom were led to stand beneath the wedding canopy. The groom wore a colorful robe and a brightly embroidered *kippah* on his head. The bride, as was the custom, was covered from head to foot in a heavily layered veil. The young man took her hand and placed the ring on her finger. "With this ring, you become my wife, and I promise to cherish you always according to the laws of Moses." At the end of the ceremony, the groom stepped on the wineglass. Now they were husband and wife.

Finally he reached the foot of the Atlas Mountains. Although he was weary, he made his way up a mountain path and found his way to a small village. It was just at sundown. The boy walked into the synagogue, where the families of the village were gathered for evening prayers. He sat in the back and waited till the prayers were over. Then he walked forward to the *bimah*, near the ark of the Torah, and spoke to the congregation. "I am a stranger here. I have come to your village because I am looking for someone. Does anyone know who is the owner of this tallit, this Siddur, this silver ring?" And he held them up for all to see.

Far in the back, in the darkening shadows, a man stood up and walked forward. "Those belong to me," he said, "but I gave them up long ago. Who are you and how did you find them?"

And the boy said, "Father, it is I—your son. You gave them to my mother, long ago. Don't you remember? I've come all this way to find you. Please come home."

The man stared at the boy. It was impossible, but it was true. This was his son. He sat down and said, "I can never go back there. Long ago I left, never to return."

The boy held his hand. "Please, you must come home, for Mother is the wisest and most beautiful of all women."

And the man thought. Maybe it's true. Maybe a miracle has taken place? "Go, my son," he said. "Walk ahead and I will follow."

And so the boy bid his father good-bye and set off back down the road to Rabat, to bring his mother the news. It was night now. The moon rose and cast its shadows on the twisting paths. A mountain stream rushed over rocks and seemed to beckon to him: "Follow me, follow me, this is the way home!" The boy walked on, but at midnight he grew weary and lay down to rest at the foot of a tall eucalyptus tree. In a deep sleep, a dream came to him. And in this dream, there appeared Elijah, of blessed memory. Elijah who heals the sick and brings messages of peace and justice to the world.

Elijah, dressed in a shining robe, spoke to the boy with soft and comforting words. "Continue on your journey, my child. But when you awake here, take the leaves from this eucalyptus tree and mix them with water from the mountain stream. Give it to your mother and let her wash in these waters. And may God's blessing be with you both."

At dawn the boy woke up. "I thought someone spoke to me," he said to himself, "but no one is here now." He was preparing to move on, when he saw something at the foot of the tree, winking in the early morning light. It was a bottle made of pure crystal. Then the boy knew that the words he had heard in the night were true. Quickly he pulled leaves from the hanging branches of the tree, crumbled them in his hand, and put them in the bottle. Then he rushed to the stream and filled it with the pure and flowing water.

"Now I'm ready to go home!" he cried to himself, and his feet almost flew as he left the mountains and made his way back to the coast, to Rabat. When he reached the door of his house, his grandfather and grandmother ran to greet him. "Take me to Mother!" he cried, and they brought him into the study.

"Mother, Mother, I have found Father. He is coming

soon. And on the way home I had a dream. It was Elijah the Prophet who came and spoke to me, I am sure of it. And look, here is a gift from him. Wash your face, quickly, for the waters are blessed."

Slowly, the woman with the face of a donkey took the bottle from her son's hands. She lifted the bottle, and poured the pure waters and fragrant leaves onto the palms of her hands. Slowly, gently, she rubbed them over her face. Then she looked up and took her hands away from her face. She was transformed. There stood a woman whose skin shone like burnished copper. Long dark hair flowed down her back, and her eyes shone with wisdom and a great light.

At that moment, a knock was heard at the door of the scholar's house. A man stood there, tired and dusty from his long travels. The scholar greeted him and led him into the study. "It is I," the man said. "I've come home at last."

Husband and wife embraced and wept with joy. The scholar and his wife thanked God that the curse of the djinn had been broken forever. The boy said, "It was Elijah! Elijah brought the miracle!" His mother and father looked at him as they gathered closely together. "Elijah helped," they said, "but the person who made the miracle come true—was you!"

And so they lived in peace, honor, and contentment till the end of their days. The blessings of Elijah stayed with them always, and so may it be with you.

THE BEAR IN THE FOREST

Once in the countryside near the town of Bialystok in Poland, a wine merchant named Reb Hershel lived in a fine and comfortable home with his wife, Libka. They were a happy couple in all ways, except one. They had no children. Once a year, Hershel and Libka would travel into the city to visit their *rebbe*, a wise teacher and leader, who could guide them in the ways of the Torah.

Long lines of petitioners were always outside the rebbe's door, seeking his help and blessings. Hershel and Libka always waited patiently until it was their turn to speak to him. Always the rebbe would have kind words of advice and comfort for them, but several years passed in this way and still no child had been born. One year, after the holiday of *Sukkot* had ended, Hershel decided to go see the rebbe by himself. This time, he put his request in writing. "Please, Rebbe, tell us when a child will be born. We need your blessing."

That day, he was invited to the front of the line outside the rebbe's door. The rebbe, dressed in a satin robe, sat in his study and beckoned Hershel to enter. He stroked his beard and said, "Reb Hershel, for many years I have watched you and Libka come to my door to ask for words of advice from me. Now I will tell you that in early summer, soon after the

holy days of *Shavuot* have ended, you and your wife will be blessed with a child. He will be healthy and strong. There is only one condition that must be fulfilled, if you wish to see your child grow into manhood."

"What is that, Rebbe?" cried Hershel. "I'll do anything to have the joy of a child growing up in my house."

The rebbe continued, "When the boy is eight days old, you will bring him into the covenant between God and Israel, as the Law requires. Make sure that on that day anyone who comes to your house, whether he be a prince or a poor and needy person, will be honored as your guest."

"Of course," said Hershel. "All will be as you say." And he rode home to bring Libka the good news.

And all did go as the rebbe had said. The holidays passed through the seasons of the year; *Hanukkah,* the Festival of Lights; *Purim* and the reading of the Book of Esther; Passover, the Festival of Freedom; and in early summer, there came Shavuot, the holiday that celebrates the Giving of the Books of the Law on Mount Sinai. A few days after the holiday had ended, Libka gave birth to a beautiful and healthy baby boy.

When the infant was eight days old, Hershel invited all his family, aunts, uncles, cousins, and friends, to his house for the ceremony. It was on that day that the boy would be named. All gathered to say the blessings over the newborn and, as was the custom, a special chair, beautifully carved and adorned with a velvet cushion, was placed near the child and his family. This was the Chair of Elijah—to ensure his blessings for a new member of the community of Israel. The parents named the baby Berel, after Hershel's own great-grandfather.

After the blessings, Hershel called everyone into the dining hall for the feast. The guests sat and ate, chattering with laughter. Everyone took a turn to come and see the baby as Libka rocked him in his cradle. Suddenly, Hershel heard a loud tapping at the door. He went to open it. He saw there a scrawny, bedraggled beggar. His shoulders were bent and he leaned heavily on his wooden walking staff. "Hershel, I've heard of your hospitality. I've come to give my blessing to your newborn and to join your feast. Put me at the head of the table, so I can see all your happy guests."

Hershel was horrified. The words of the rebbe and his promise flew out of his head. "How can I let this dirty man into the house?" he muttered to himself. "My family and friends will be insulted to sit with him." But the beggar pounded his staff at the door. "Hershel, I insist, I must sit at the head of the table and give *my* blessings to the child."

Reluctantly, Hershel led him into the dining hall. Quickly he pushed a low stool toward the back of the room. "Here"— he gestured—"why don't you sit there. One of my servants will bring you all the food you need."

The beggar stared at him a moment and then he said, "Let us see what your wife has to say about this."

The beggar made his way to the head of the table. "Libka, my dear, I have heard the happy news. I'm a stranger to you, I know, but I, too, would like to give my blessings to your newborn. Let me sit at the head of the table, so I can enjoy the feast. I've traveled from afar to be here."

Libka stared at him and then burst out laughing. "I hardly think," she said, "that a *schnorrer* like you is welcome here. Go, take a few scraps if you want, and then be off with you!"

The beggar turned away slowly. He made his way to the back of the room and sat on the stool that Hershel had offered him. He neither ate nor drank anything that the servant offered to him, but before the guests began to leave, he stood up and reached into his pocket. Silently, he walked over to the door and pulled out a piece of white chalk. The chalk squeaked over the heavy wood as he scratched out his message on the door. The guests held their ears. Hershel and Libka watched in dismay. What could he be doing?

The beggar turned around once and then walked out the door and quickly away, the loud tapping of his staff fading into soft echoes on the road. But in the doorway the words he had written were plain for all to see:

BEREL THE BEAR SHALL LIVE.

Libka and Hershel rushed to the door. They tried to find the beggar, but he was gone. They ran back to the door and tried to rub out the words, but the chalk letters didn't erase. They took soap and water. They washed, they rubbed, and they scrubbed, but the letters grew even clearer and brighter. Finally they gave up. The words remained. All the guests left, wondering what was the meaning of this strange event.

At first, Berel seemed like any ordinary child. At six months he sat and smiled. At a year he crawled. But when he began to walk, his parents noticed a soft downy fur that began to grow on his back and over his arms and his legs. He never wanted to stay indoors, but spent all his time outside the house near the woods. As he grew, his nose turned into a snout, his hands into paws with long claws. The only kind of food he would eat was nuts and berries. His parents called all the greatest doctors from near and far to see him, but nothing helped. On the day of his seventh birthday, Berel ran into the forest and never returned.

Six years passed. One night, Hershel and Libka were awakened by a scratching sound at the door. Hershel went down the stairs to see who was there. The door was open, but no one was in sight. He ran to see if a thief had stolen any of his precious possessions, but everything was exactly as it always was. Then Hershel saw a book, lying open on the table. He had never seen the book before. Its pages were trimmed with gold leaf and it was bound in finest leather. The wind blew the first page of the book open, and he read the words that were written there in golden ink:

"Father, I am thirteen years old. Now that I am a Bar Mitzvah, a grown man, I need my own *tefillin* and prayer shawl, so that I can pray as the commandments teach us." The page was signed with a paw print.

Hershel took the book and the very next day rode into Bialystok and showed it to the rebbe. "Rebbe, my son has become a wild thing, a bear who lives in the forest. Yet he leaves me this message. What should I do?"

The rebbe stroked his beard. "You must give him everything he asked for. Don't you remember the words on your door? Berel the Bear shall live!"

And so that night, Hershel placed a set of tefillin and a woven prayer shawl on the table in the study. The wind blew hard that night. The branches of the trees rattled against the windows. Hershel and Libka hardly slept a wink. In the morning, when they went downstairs, the door to the study once again was open. And the tefillin and prayer shawl were gone.

Six years passed again. During all that time, they heard nothing from Berel. But on the night of his eighteenth birthday, Hershel and Libka once again heard a scratching at the door. They went downstairs to see who was there. Again, the door was open but the house was empty.

Lying on the table, the book with golden pages was open once again. They rushed to find the words that had been written, again in gold ink. "Father and Mother, I'm eighteen years old. Now it is time for me to marry. Please find a proper maiden to be my wife."

The very next day, Hershel rode into Bialystok to consult with his rebbe. "Rebbe," he said, "this time what Berel has asked for is impossible. How will I ever find a maiden to marry him? He is a bear!"

The rebbe did not answer at first. Then he took a quill pen and wrote a few words on a small piece of paper.

"Reb Hershel. You must do as your son requests. Follow the directions I have written here for you. Go to the city of Cracow. Find the man whose name is written here, and his family. It may take you a long time. It may take you no time at all. But do not rest until you find him. You must stay with him for the whole Sabbath. Do not leave his house for any reason. And if you see anything that is strange or unusual, do not say a word to him until the Sabbath is over and the first three stars appear in the sky. Berel shall live. Now go."

Hershel obeyed the rebbe's words. He ordered his coachman to take him on the long journey to Cracow. When he reached the city, he opened the paper to look at the name of the man written there—"Schmerel the Pauper" was all the paper said. Reb Hershel went from person to person to ask if anyone knew of Schmerel the Pauper. "Oh, Schmerel, he's the poorest man in the city, but we don't know where he lives."

Hershel had almost given up hope when an old woman selling bread on the street corner called him over.

"Are you looking for Schmerel the Pauper? I can tell you where he lives." She pointed down a narrow street filled with mud and strewn with scraps of wood and garbage. Hershel left his coachman behind and told him to wait in the square until he returned. Holding his nose, he made his way down the narrow street. At the very end, when he thought he had reached the edge of the city and could go no farther, he saw a ramshackle little house, barely standing on its spindly foundation.

Hershel took off his hat and knocked on the door. It was Friday, late afternoon, just before the Sabbath. With a creak, the door opened, and there stood Schmerel himself. His cheeks were sunken and his hands shook, but he welcomed Hershel into the house. "Good sir, it's rare that I have visitors here. How can I help you?"

Reb Hershel replied, "I am a stranger in Cracow. I'm only looking for a place to stay the night and celebrate the Sabbath."

Schmerel laughed. "I would be honored to have you as a guest, but as you can see we are poor here. I don't have a bed for you to rest on, much less a proper meal to feed you. My wife and I live here from hand to mouth."

"Never mind about that," Hershel said. "I can provide for all our needs."

Schmerel then welcomed him in with joy. Hershel sent a message to his coachman, who soon returned with a downy mattress and food and drink—enough to celebrate the Sabbath meal three times over.

Schmerel's wife set about to cook the dinner. She lit the Sabbath candles and said the blessings over them. Hershel was given the honor of saying the *Kiddush*, the blessing over the wine. As they sat down to enjoy their meal, Hershel noticed that the table was set for ten. This puzzled him, but he did not say a word. This time he remembered the rebbe's warning. Schmerel and his wife served out portions for each of them. She also filled the seven empty plates. Then she carried them, one by one, behind a small door that opened into their tiny kitchen. Hershel waited for an explanation but none was offered.

The following day, after morning prayers, she set out a meal, and once again carried seven plates behind the small door. Hershel was silent and didn't ask any questions. But after the last meal had been served this way, and the evening stars rose in the sky, he jumped up and asked, "Now, Reb Schmerel, what is the meaning of these strange goings on? Where have you and your wife been taking all the food?"

Schmerel sighed. "Reb Hershel, I'll tell you the truth. My wife and I were blessed with children. Seven beautiful daughters. But as you can see, the wheels of fortune have not turned well for me. My daughters have no clothes to wear, and so we keep them in the attic up the stairs behind the kitchen."

"I must speak to your daughters," said Reb Hershel. "It is of greatest importance to my family." Immediately he called his coachman again and bade him bring three trunks full of embroidered dresses, scarves, and hats for Schmerel's children. In a short time the coachman returned. Schmerel's wife took the clothes up into the attic.

As soon as the young women were dressed, Hershel asked to see them. One at a time, they came down the attic stairs. Masha, the first daughter, greeted him, and thanked him for his generosity. Then he spoke. "Young woman, I have an only son. I am looking for a bride. Would you care to marry him?"

Masha said, "I would be glad to marry him. But first, can you tell me anything about him? What is he like?"

Hershel only shook his head. "No," he said, "that I cannot do."

Then Masha replied, "How can I marry someone I know nothing about? That is no match for me." And she sat down at the kitchen table.

Next came Basha, then Bayla, Rayzel, Rivka, and Pesha. To each one he asked the question, and from each he got the same reply. How could they marry someone they knew nothing about?

The last to come down the stairs was Tsiveh. She had soft brown eyes and hair as black as midnight. When she spoke her voice was strong. "Many thanks for the new dresses," said she. "Now at last I don't have to stay in my parents' attic!"

"Tsiveh, I have an only son, " said Hershel. "Would you care to be his wife?"

all become my friends. Every day I study the Torah with Elijah, and Talmud and *Midrash*, too. He feeds me and cares for me, as if I were his own son. So I have grown. On the day of the wedding, I will come as a bear. If you still care to marry me, wait until I step on the wineglass and all will go well for us."

Tsiveh was astonished at what she was seeing. Yet she knew in her heart this was the companion that God had chosen for her. "Yes," she said, "I will marry you."

Berel smiled. "Don't tell anyone," he said, "until the day of the wedding. Keep it a secret. But if you must, your sisters can know, if they come to this house as my father's guests."

The next day, the wedding guests began to arrive. Tsiveh looked out the window and watched them come — in carriages and coaches, on foot and on horseback. The very last to arrive were her mother, her father, and her sisters.

Before the ceremony began, Tsiveh ran to greet them. "Sisters," she said, "you will see something strange today at the wedding. My bridegroom is not what he appears. Don't be frightened by anything you see — for I know that all will be well."

As the wedding began, Hershel and Libka stood with the young servant underneath the canopy. Tsiveh, in bridal veil and gown, was led to greet him. Seven times she circled around him. The rebbe himself stood with them and chanted the seven blessings for the bride and groom.

Suddenly, a great bear pushed his way through the crowd and roared up to the bride. The servant was bowled over, and before another word could be said, the bear placed a ring on the bride's finger and stepped on the wineglass. He and the bride ran to the carriage that was waiting and immediately the horse sped away, leaving Hershel and Libka and all the guests gasping in surprise and wonder.

No sooner had the carriage left the grounds of his father's house than Berel's fur slipped entirely away. His bear hide never returned, for now he was fully human. And so he and Tsiveh found their way to a new town on the other side of the country. He became a scholar, known for his wisdom and knowledge. And she became a great storyteller. For miles around, people would come to study with Berel and to hear Tsiveh's tales of magic and wonder.

And every so often, in the house of Hershel the wine merchant and his wife Libka in Bialystok, a new page in the book of fine leather would be found open. The page would be filled with words in golden ink, as if some unseen hand had written them. But the end of the page was always signed, "Your son, Berel, who lives in happiness and contentment."

And so it was, till the book was completed, and the end of their days had come.

7
THE STRANGE JOURNEY OF RABBI JOSHUA BEN LEVI

Many centuries ago, in the town of Lydda in ancient Palestine, there lived a rabbi named Joshua ben Levi. He was one of the most learned of all the scholars of his time. From an early age, he studied the Torah and the Talmud. He could quote and argue the Law better than almost anyone. If a young student or visiting scholar had a question, they would come to Rabbi Joshua and he always knew how to guide them to the right and sensible answer.

But Rabbi Joshua was not content. All of his studying still did not give him the knowledge of the world that he sought. "I need to study with a great teacher," he said to himself, "someone who can lead me to true understanding and wisdom."

Rabbi Joshua had heard many legends of how the Prophet Elijah had visited great scholars of the past. Of course, Rabbi Joshua knew that Elijah had traveled up into heaven on a chariot of fire and that he hadn't died as ordinary people do. But he also knew that Elijah could still appear on earth. "I won't be content until I, too, can study with Elijah the Prophet. Only then will I learn what I need to know of the ways of the world."

So Rabbi Joshua began to pray. He prayed and he

prayed. For seven days and seven nights, he did not touch any food. He drank only water from an underground spring. All that time, he was praying that Elijah would come down from heaven and be his teacher.

On the eighth day, Elijah finally did appear. "Rabbi Joshua," he said, "your prayers have been so strong, they traveled right up to heaven. I had to come and speak to you. Why do you want me to be your teacher?"

And Joshua said, "I've learned all that I can from books. If I could travel with you and see the world as you do, I could learn even more—for I want the keys to wisdom and understanding of life on earth."

Elijah sighed. "Rabbi Joshua, I would give you permission to come with me, but a scholar like you could not stand to see the strange and terrible things you will witness on such a journey."

Rabbi Joshua pleaded with him, and finally Elijah said, "Rabbi Joshua, I know you have an inquisitive mind. Besides, your constant prayers were disturbing the angels' rest. So I will grant your request. You may go traveling with me. But if you have any questions about what you witness, you must keep your thoughts to yourself. If you speak to me about anything that you see, your journey with me will have to come to an end."

Rabbi Joshua was overjoyed. Elijah had answered his prayers! He promised to keep silent. "Just let me pack my bags," he said, "and I'll be ready to go."

And in a few minutes, Rabbi Joshua was standing at

Elijah's side, a small pack on his back and a walking stick in his hand, just as Elijah had.

They walked together down the road for some time. As the night grew cold, they came upon a small cottage in the distance. Coming closer, Elijah knocked on the door. The door opened and there stood a farmer and his wife. They welcomed in the weary travelers and gave them a simple but satisfying meal of soup and bread. Since there were no extra beds in the house, the farmer and his wife offered their own cots to Rabbi Joshua and Elijah, while they slept outside in the small barn that housed a few goats, some sheep, and their one prize cow.

In the morning, they gave the travelers another good meal and bade them farewell. As they walked past the barn, Rabbi Joshua heard Elijah mutter under his breath, "May the cow in the barn die tomorrow."

Rabbi Joshua was amazed. "Those people were so kind to us," he said. "How could you wish for their prize cow to die?"

Elijah looked at Joshua. "Remember what I told you," he said. "You must watch and listen. You may think what you wish, but don't ask questions, or our journey together will have to end." So Rabbi Joshua kept his peace.

They continued on their way until they reached the house of a prosperous landowner. It was almost nightfall. The two weary travelers knocked on the door. A servant opened it, but told them that there was no room for them in the house.

"Our master cannot be troubled by visitors today,"

the servant said. "He has instructed me to tell any travelers who stop by to go and sleep in the shed by the walls of our mansion."

And so Elijah and Joshua had to sleep outside in the cold, drafty shed. At dawn, as they prepared to take their leave, Elijah saw that one of the walls surrounding the house was broken and in need of repair. "May this wall be rebuilt so that it stands for generations to come!" And instantly the wall straightened, its bricks replaced and cemented in a perfect line, strong and sturdy. Rabbi Joshua was about to speak again, but this time he kept his thoughts to himself. Still he was deeply puzzled. Why did this landowner who kept us out in the cold receive this reward?

Nevertheless, he picked up his bag and followed Elijah down the road. They walked and walked until they came within sight of a town. When they drew nearer, they saw that every house in the town was built of solid stone. Streets were bustling with merchants and shopkeepers selling their wares. They walked into the town hall and saw that each seat was engraved with the name of its owner, painted in silver and gold. That day, the hall was filled with the town's most important citizens.

As the Prophet Elijah and his companion entered and walked through the crowd, one of the townspeople turned his head and said, "Who will feed these strangers who have come to our town tonight?"

His neighbor said, "Why should we feed them? Let them look after themselves! Water and salt will be enough for them!" And they burst out laughing. Soon the whole group gathered there were laughing and pointing fingers at Elijah and Joshua. "Water and salt—that's all you need to get by!"

Elijah only waved and nodded his head. Then he motioned to Rabbi Joshua. They turned and walked out the door, the laughter still echoing in their ears. As they walked through the streets of the city, Rabbi Joshua heard Elijah say, "May everyone in this town become a leader!"

"May everyone in this town became a—?" Rabbi Joshua almost burst out shouting, but he stopped himself in time and kept silent. In his thoughts, he was boiling with arguments and questions for Elijah. Why should anyone in this town of selfish people become a leader?

They kept on walking. The sun was setting and evening began to fall. Tired and hungry, they followed a muddy path that led to a small village. The roofs in this small town were all thatched with straw, and Rabbi Joshua saw the humble clothing and dress that the people wore. Still, it wasn't long before a villager walked up to them and said, "Welcome, strangers, you look tired and hungry."

Another man came over to them and said, "Our houses are small, it's true, but we always have room somewhere in town for weary travelers." And soon, friendly folk led them to shelter for the night.

In the morning, all the villagers came to bid Rabbi Joshua and Elijah farewell, and even gave them a basket of bread and meat for their journey. As they made their way back down the muddy path that led to the main road, Elijah said, "May the people in this town have only one leader!"

Finally, Rabbi Joshua could not contain himself anymore.

"This is really too much!" he said. "Come what may, I demand to know the meaning of all your strange actions."

"Why," said Elijah, "what do you mean?"

"The first couple we met gave us food and shelter for the night and even left their own beds to give us a place to sleep—yet you asked for their cow to die! But the landowner who kept us out all night in a shed, you rewarded by building a new wall."

"Rabbi Joshua," said Elijah, "are you sure you want to keep speaking? You know what this means."

But Rabbi Joshua continued. "Our journey may end, but not until you explain to me why you prayed for that town of selfish people to have many leaders while for this village we have just left, where the people gave us food and shelter, you wished for only one leader. What is the meaning of all of this?"

Elijah put down his walking stick. "Rabbi Joshua," he said, "you have studied from all the holy books. You say you wish for the keys to wisdom and understanding of life on earth. The first key to wisdom is to realize that all that you see is not what it seems." Then he clapped his hands. The stick turned into a tall tree with leaves that sprouted flowers of gold and silver. He clapped his hands again and the stick turned into a flying dove, carrying a twig in its beak. He clapped his hands a third time and the stick turned into a stream of water that bubbled and rushed past their feet. Only when he clapped his hands for the last time did the stick return to its original shape and size. Rabbi Joshua stood back in awe.

"You have asked me to answer your questions," Elijah said, "and now I will answer them for you—only know that when I come to the end of the story, so will our journey together end."

And Elijah began to speak. "When we visited the farmer and his wife who were so kind to us, I knew that in heaven it had been decreed that the farmer's life would end the very next day. And so I prayed that their prize cow would die in his place. As for the landowner who kept us outside in the cold, I knew that underneath his broken wall there was buried a great treasure: a chest full of gold, diamonds, and silver. And so I prayed for the wall to be built there strong and secure. He will never reap the greatest reward from his land.

"As for the two towns we visited," Elijah said, "have you ever heard the proverb 'A ship with too many captains will surely sink'? In the same way, a community that has too many leaders will never find peace and harmony. There will be arguing and discontent among them. Life will become hard for them, until they learn how to change their ways. Another proverb says, 'Even the strongest tree can grow from only one seed.' The small village we have just left will soon have one true leader to guide and help them. In days to come, their fortunes will change and their town will grow and prosper for many generations. These are the things, Rabbi Joshua, that cannot be learned from any book. Only by asking your heart to look beyond what you see, will you come nearer to the knowledge and understanding that you seek. Things are not always what they seem. Remember these words, and learn what you can from them."

Rabbi Joshua nodded his head. He was beginning to understand.

"I must leave you now," said his teacher, "for our journey together has come to an end."

Elijah tapped his stick on the ground and walked up the road. Slowly he disappeared from sight. Only the sound of his words remained, echoing in the still morning air, until they, too, faded in the breeze. Rabbi Joshua returned to his home in Lydda, thinking all the time about what he had seen and heard. As the years passed, he became known not only for his great knowledge, but also for a special wisdom and understanding of the ways of the world, which he shared with others till the end of his days.

8
WHERE IS ELIJAH?

Simon Fischkoff was a jeweler by trade. Back in the early 1900s, his own mother and father had come to America in the ships crowded with immigrants leaving their home and family in Russia far behind.

At first, they lived on the Lower East Side of Manhattan in a crowded tenement, but soon after Simon was born they decided to cross over the East River and raise their children in the borough of Brooklyn. So Simon grew up there, playing stickball in the streets of Ocean Parkway with his brothers. On weekends he would walk on the brightly lit sidewalks of Brighton Beach and Coney Island. Even though he spoke mostly English and went to public schools, his mother and father raised him to follow the ways of the Jewish tradition that they themselves had learned as children in Odessa.

Simon's favorite holiday was Passover. He would help his mother clean the house and polish the silverware till it shone. For the eight days of Passover, no bread was allowed in the house; only the unleavened bread, the matzah, could be eaten. The night before Passover, he would walk with his father through the house by candlelight to search out every last crumb of bread. He knew his mother would always leave some in the corners, so that he, Simon, could sweep them up with her feather broom.

The next day, Simon's mother and father, his grandmother and grandfather, and his two brothers would gather at the table for the Seder, the festival meal. He loved to hear his grandfather read from the *Haggadah*, the Passover book that told the story of how Moses led the Jewish people out of slavery in Egypt to freedom. He would listen to his youngest brother ask the four questions. "Why is this night different from all other nights?" the littlest one chanted, just as Simon had done when he was the youngest child.

While the grown-ups were eating, Simon and his brothers would search through the house, looking for the *afikoman*, the last piece of matzah which his father had hidden secretly sometime during the Seder. Whoever found the matzah could bargain for it with his father at the end of the meal. But Simon's favorite part of the Seder meal was when his mother would say, "Go open the door. It's time to let in Elijah!" Then he would run to the door, while his father held up the Cup of Elijah, the silver goblet, polished best of all. With song and prayer, they would welcome in their honored guest.

It always seemed to Simon that the wineglass was a little emptier when he went back to close the door. Had Elijah really come?

Simon went to school and grew up. As a young man, he learned to cut diamonds and gems. Every day, he would ride the subway and cross the Brooklyn Bridge to Manhattan, where he would work hard at his trade. Then, in the evening, with the sun setting over New York harbor, he would make his way back home again. Simon married, too, and began to raise his own children.

Every year at Passover, the family would gather in his apartment for the Seder. Simon would raise the Kiddush cup and say the blessing for the beginning of the holiday. He taught his youngest son the four questions, and he always hid the matzah, just as his father had done.

Every year, the family opened the door and held up the silver goblet, the Cup of Elijah, that his parents had handed down to him, and they would sing, "In our days, come among us and bring the Messiah, Son of David."

Years passed. Simon's own children grew up. And one day before Passover Eve, he realized he had a question. A question that had been bothering him for some time. He put on his hat and walked down the street to see the rabbi who led the services in the small synagogue near his house.

He knocked on the the door of the rabbi's study. The rabbi beckoned him in. "Simon, I hope all is well," said the rabbi. "How is the family? What can I do for you today?"

"Rabbi," said Simon, "I've lived in Brooklyn my whole life. I've kept the traditions of the Jewish people and taught them to my children. For over forty years, I have observed the Passover and read the Haggadah as the Law says, 'And you shall tell it to your children, in every generation.' Rabbi, I have done all these things, but I have a question that has been nagging me for a long time."

"Tell me your question," said the rabbi gently.

"Rabbi, for forty years I've been opening the door for

Elijah, but I have never seen him! What does Elijah really look like? How would I know him if I ever did see him? Surely somewhere in our books of knowledge there is an answer to my question."

The rabbi rocked back in his chair. "Simon," he said, "you want to see Elijah. I will tell you now, there is a way you can see him."

Simon drew close to listen. The rabbi began, "You know the Yakovich family — they have just immigrated here from Russia?"

"Yes, I know them," said Simon.

"They arrived here with just the clothes on their backs. Their apartment is bare and empty and they hardly know how to take care of themselves yet."

"Yes," Simon said. "Yes, I know."

"Then, Simon," said the rabbi, "tomorrow I want you to go to the Yakovichs' apartment. Give them everything they need for the Seder meal. Sit with them and sing the holiday songs with them and take care of them for all the eight days of the holiday. I promise you that on Passover night, you will see Elijah walking in their door."

Simon thanked the rabbi and walked quickly home. He told his wife to hurry, they must prepare many things to bring to the Yakovichs' house.

That night, he and his wife sat with the newly arrived family. They brought candles and wine, matzah and charoset, a whole roast chicken, and a Haggadah for everyone at the table. He sat and taught them the holiday songs and how to read the four questions. Simon made sure that not only on the first night, but on every night of Passover, the Yakovich family was well taken care of.

At the end of the eight days, he went back to his rabbi. Softly, he knocked on the door.

"Rabbi," said Simon, "I did everything you told me. I spent the holiday with the Yakovich family and made sure they had food and wine every night. We gave them our Haggadah books and taught them about the four questions. We followed every part of the Seder with them, but Rabbi, I never saw Elijah!"

The rabbi smiled and reached over to a drawer near his desk. "Simon," he said, "I know that Elijah did come to your Seder this year. But of course, you couldn't see him."

And with that he put a small mirror into Simon's hand.

"Look closely and you will see, my friend. This was the face of Elijah that night."

GLOSSARY

Many of the words in this book come from other languages. Sometimes, even in English, these words are pronounced differently depending on who is speaking and where they come from. The following guide will help you to pronounce the words that may not be familiar to you. In Hebrew or Yiddish, "ch" is pronounced like the ending sound of the word "yech!"

afikoman (ah-fee-KOH-mahn) Originally from ancient Greek, this is a word that means, literally, "dessert." At Passover, it is the piece of matzah, or unleavened bread, which must be eaten at the end of the ritual meal. In most Jewish homes, it is a custom for an adult to hide this piece of matzah, which the children must later find and bring back to the Seder table.

agunah (ah-GOO-nah) A Hebrew word for a deserted wife. According to Jewish law, a woman whose husband deserts her cannot remarry unless she has proof of his death or is able to obtain an official divorce from a rabbinical court.

alef-bet (ah-lehf beh-t) The Hebrew word for "alphabet." There are twenty-two letters in the Hebrew alphabet. All studies in Jewish education begin with the learning of these letters.

B.C.E. Before the Common Era, equivalent to B.C.

Bar Mitzvah (bar-MITS-vah) A Hebrew word that means "son of the commandments." It is the name for the coming-of-age ceremony of young boys in the Jewish tradition. At a Bar Mitzvah, a thirteen-year-old boy stands before the congregation and reads aloud a portion of the Torah. At this time, he is considered old enough to take on the responsibility of carrying out the "mitzvot"—the commandments of the Torah. In recent times, a similar ceremony for girls, called Bat Mitzvah (daughter of the commandments) has been instituted in many synagogues and congregations.

berel (BEH-rel) A Yiddish word which literally means "bear."

Bialystok (bee-AH-lih-stock) A city in northeastern Poland which, up to the Holocaust era, was known as a center of Jewish learning and culture. Remnants of the Jewish community, its synagogues and buildings, can still be found in present-day Bialystok.

bimah (BEE-mah) The Hebrew word for the area of the synagogue (usually a raised platform) from which the Torah scrolls are read.

C.E. Common Era, equivalent to A.D.

Chair of Elijah In the Jewish tradition, it became a custom to place a chair for Elijah near the godfather at the *brit milah*, which literally means "covenant." These chairs are often carved and decorated with ornate designs. This custom grew out of a belief that Elijah is a guardian of newborn infants, and a special blessing is said in his honor.

challah (KHAH-lah) A loaf of braided bread, over which a blessing is said on Friday evenings as part of the Sabbath home ritual.

charoset (kha-ROH-set) A mixture of sweet fruits (such as apples or dates), spices, wine, and nuts served as part of the Passover ceremony.

cheder (KHAY-dehr) The Yiddish word for a school of Jewish learning. Since Jews often lived in countries where their traditions were not taught in the official schools, the cheder was the place where the richness and complexity of Jewish religious thought, law, and prayer were passed on to successive generations.

Cracow A large city in the south of Poland where a Jewish community was established as early as the fourteenth century.

Cup of Elijah The Cup of Elijah is another important symbol in Jewish home ritual, as an integral part of the Passover Seder. It is often made with special designs and exquisite craftsmanship. Traditionally, the Cup of Elijah is left full as if in anticipation of the arrival of an honored guest.

dinar (dee-NAHR) An ancient coin of the Middle East, usually made of silver or gold.

djinn (jih-n) In Arabic folklore, a spirit that can take different forms. Some of the djinn are kind and helpful, while others are malicious. In Arab lands, there was substantial cultural borrowing between the Jewish community and neighboring peoples. Folkloric expressions and beliefs were part of that process of cultural exchange, which occurred over many generations.

fellah (FELL-ah) An Arabic word used in Egypt for a farmer or peasant who works the land.

Haggadah (hah-GAH-dah) The Hebrew word for the book of stories, songs, and prayers that are read at the Passover meal. The focus of the Haggadah is to tell and remember the Exodus from Egypt and the deliverance of the Jewish people from slavery. Although every Hagaddah shares common elements, there are many different versions of this book, which has been shaped by the diverse communities within Jewish culture and civilization.

hamsin (hahm-SEEN) The Arabic word for the hot winds that blow out of the Sahara Desert, across the Middle East and toward the Mediterranean, causing heat waves at different times throughout the year.

Hanukkah (HAH-noo-kah) The eight-day Festival of Lights, celebrated in early winter, to commemorate the Jewish victory over a Syrian-Greek army and the rededication of the Holy Temple in Jerusalem, which occurred in the third century B.C.E.

Havdalah (hahv-DAH-lah) The Hebrew word for the weekly ceremony that marks the end of the Sabbath (every Saturday night) and the beginning of the secular days of the week. This ceremony begins when the first three stars are spotted in the evening sky. A braided candle is lit and sweet spices are passed around to every member of the family. It is at this ceremony that a hymn to Elijah is sung. The words of the hymn express the hope that this week the Messiah will come.

kaffiyeh (kah-FEE-yuh) The word for the woven cloth head-wrapping traditionally worn by men in many countries of the Arab-speaking world.

kiddush (KIH-desh) The prayer spoken over a cup of wine at the beginning of the Sabbath and other holy days. It comes from the Hebrew verb kadesh, which means "to sanctify."

kippah (kee-PAH) The Hebrew word for the small, round cap worn by observant Jews (usually men). The Yiddish word for this cap is yarmulkah. Wearing a kippah symbolizes the person's respect for God and is a reminder to the wearer to keep the commandments of the Torah and Jewish law.

Loire Valley An area in the central part of France that takes its name from the Loire River. This area is known for its rich farmlands and stately castles that have stood there since the time of the Crusades.

Lydda A city of ancient Palestine, located on the coastal plain, now the modern town of Lod in Israel.

Marrakech (Mah-rah-kesh) A city known as a center for trade and commerce in southern Morocco near the Atlas Mountains.

matzah (mahtz-ah) The flat, thin, unleavened bread that is an important part of the Seder meal at Passover.

melamed (meh-LAH-med) Both a Hebrew and a Yiddish word for a teacher of the Hebrew language and Jewish studies. Usually the term refers to a teacher of children.

Messiah A word with many different meanings depending on the culture or religion it is used by. In the Jewish tradition, a belief in the Messiah developed in the second century B.C.E. At that time, the land of Judea was under attack and invasion by many hostile armies. It was believed that a royal prince from the house of King David would appear to liberate Judea and bring about universal peace and justice for all peoples. The belief in the the Messiah continued to be strongly held in different Jewish communities during the centuries of the Diaspora, and it continues to the present day.

Midrash From the Hebrew word that means "to explain, to draw out." A midrash is a rabbinic tale or legend used to explain, interpret, or embellish passages from the Torah.

Odessa (oh-DEH-sah) A city in southeastern Russia near the Black Sea. From the 1800's to the 1920's, it was the home of one of the largest Jewish communities in Russia.

Purim (poor-eem) The Jewish holiday that falls in late winter or early spring. The focus of this joyous holiday is the reading of the Book of Esther. On Purim, children dress up as the different characters in the story and in other costumes. In synagogue, it is a custom to bring noisemakers to "wipe out" the name of Haman, the villain of the story, whenever it is spoken by the reader.

Rabat (rah-BAHT) A city on the coast of Morocco, now its capital. The Jewish community had been long established in Morocco, and Rabat was one of its centers of commerce and learning.

reb The Yiddish word for "mister."

rebbe (reb-beh) A Yiddish word for a specially honored spiritual teacher or religious leader.

Salaam Aley-kum (sah-lahm ah-LAY-koom) The phrase of greeting in Arabic, which literally means "peace be unto you" (see Shalom Aleichem).

Schmerel (shmeh-rehl) The Yiddish form of the Hebrew name Shemaryah, which means "protection of the Lord."

schnorrer (shnoh-rer) A Yiddish expression for a "freeloader"—someone who always finds a way to take advantage of a situation and get something, such as a meal or a place to sleep, without giving anything in return.

Seder (SAY-der) The name for the festive Passover meal, which includes songs, prayers, partaking of symbolic foods, and the retelling of the Exodus story.

Shabbat (shah-BAHT) The Sabbath, the seventh day of the week, a day of rest and prayer.

Shalom Aleichem (shah-lome ah-LAY-khem) The Hebrew greeting phrase, which literally means "peace be unto you" (see Salaam Aley-kum).

Shavuot (shah-voo-OHT) The name of the Jewish holiday that usually falls in late May or June and that commemorates the giving of the Torah at Mount Sinai.

Siddur (see-DOOR) The name for the Jewish prayer book used at home and in synagogue services.

Sukkot (soo-COAT) A holiday celebrating the fall harvest.

Talmud (TAHL-mood) From the Hebrew word that means "to study, to learn," this is the name for the extensive volumes of rabbinic law, tales, legends, and commentary on the Torah that have guided Jewish life for many centuries.

tallit (tah-leet) The Hebrew word for the ritual prayer shawl worn by observant Jews during morning prayers every day, as well as Shabbat and holidays.

tefillin (teh-FILL-in) Two small leather boxes containing scriptural passages which are bound to the left hand and forehead, worn by observant Jews during morning prayers to fulfill an ancient biblical commandment.

Torah (toh-RAH) The Five Books of Moses, the center of all Jewish belief and religious practice, which are written on parchment scrolls and read during synagogue services. The word "Torah" can also be used to refer to the other books of the Bible or, in some instances, to all of Jewish learning and study.

Tsiveh (TSIH-veh) The Yiddish form of the Hebrew name Tzivyah, which means "deer" or "gazelle."

Yakov (YAH-kove) The Hebrew word for Jacob.

Yom Kippur (yom key-POOR) The name for the Day of Atonement, the holiest day of the Jewish year, which falls during the month of September or October. Yom Kippur also signals the end of the High Holy Days period. It is observed with fasting and contemplation of one's acts and deeds of the year.

Yossel (YUH-sehl) A Yiddish form of the name Yosef, or Joseph.

Zabledov (ZAH-bleh-dove) The name of a town in Poland, south of Bialystok, which had a large Jewish community. Zabledov was destroyed during the Holocaust, but photographs of its famous fortress synagogue can be seen today in the book *Wooden Synagogues* by Maria and Kazimierz Piechotka.

ABOUT THE STORIES

INTRODUCTION

The information for the introduction was drawn from various sources. The biblical narratives relating to Elijah can be found in the Book of Kings I (17:1) and II (2:13). Elijah's character and transformation in folk literature has been written about by Professor Dov Noy, in the *Encyclopedia Judaica*'s article "Elijah" (Vol. 3, p. 638); as well as many other studies in Jewish folklore scholarship (see Weinreich and Schwartzbaum in the bibliography). The role of Elijah in ancient Near Eastern art and holy sites was discussed at length by Professor Bezalel Narkiss of the Hebrew University at a lecture on March 5, 1995, sponsored by the Center for Jewish Art in New York City. The story about Elijah holding his nose when he passed a haughty man on the road is cited in *Studies in Jewish and World Folklore* by Haim Schwartzbaum.

THE DREAM

This story is based on a theme or motif which can be found in many of the world's folktales—that of a protagonist who listens to a message in a dream and travels far, only to learn that his treasure can be found at home. It appears in Uri Shulevitz's picture book, *The Treasure*. A version can also be found in Beatrice Silverman Weinreich's book *Yiddish Folktales* under the title "The Treasure at Home." The story was also told by the

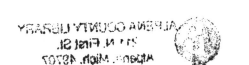

legendary Hasidic rabbi and teacher, Reb Nachman of Bratzlav (1772-1811). My own retelling was first inspired by an Irish version of the story, "The Peddler of Ballaghadereen," in Ruth Sawyer's classic book, *The Way of the Storyteller*, in which St. Patrick appears in a dream to a poor peddler. In the early 1980s, I recreated the story in an Eastern European Jewish setting and began to retell it with the characters of Reb Yakov and the Prophet Elijah. Zabledov is the name of the small town in Poland where my grandfather, Chaim Cohen, was born and raised.

ELIJAH IN THE MARKETPLACE

This story of Elijah has been recorded in Louis Ginzberg's comprehensive collection of rabbinic lore, *Legends of the Jews* (Vol. IV). Another version of it can be found in Samuel Segal's *Elijah: A Study in Jewish Folklore*, from a text by Rabbi Nissim ben Jacob that dates back to the sixteenth century. The story has also been retold by Isaac Bashevis Singer in the picture book, *Elijah the Slave*. In Jewish folklore, there are numerous tales in which Elijah appears in the guise of an Arab farmer or peasant. For this collection, the story is set in Alexandria, Egypt, where a Jewish community was in existence from the second century B.C.E.

THE THREE BROTHERS

The Ma'aseh Book by Moses Gaster is a collection of legends, folktales, and fables that were popular in the Judeo–German–speaking areas of Europe in the sixteenth and seventeenth centuries. This retelling is based on the story "Elijah and the Three Sons

Who Watched in the Garden" in the English translation of *The Ma'aseh Book*. Elijah as one who grants wishes is a motif in many folktales of the Jewish oral tradition. Another version can also be found in Louis Ginzberg's *Legends of the Jews* (Vol. IV).

ELIJAH AND THE FISHER BOY

This story is similar in form to the famous Grimm fairy tale, "The Fisherman and His Wife." In an earlier version of the tale, when the boy asks to be God, then God rebukes Elijah, saying, "Now you understand that my ways are just." A version of this story from the oral tradition of Yiddish-speaking Jews of Eastern Europe can be found in Weinreich's study, "The Prophet Elijah in Modern Yiddish Folktales," and in her collection, *Yiddish Folktales*, under the title "The Leper Boy and Elijah the Prophet."

THE WOMAN WITH THE FACE OF A DONKEY

I first encountered this tale in Howard Schwartz's collection *Miriam's Tambourine: Jewish Folktales from Around the World*, under the title "The Donkey Girl." This Moroccan Jewish tale is discussed at length in Chapter I of Aliza Shenhar's book, *Jewish and Israeli Folktales*. The story is based on a universal motif, which can be found in different forms all over the world, in which a young man or woman, placed under a curse to appear as an animal, is restored to human form through the return of a loved one. In the process known as "Judaization," the story acquired elements specific to Jewish culture, such as the characters of the scholar and young student, the gifts of the prayer shawl and prayer book, and the appearance of Elijah the Prophet.

THE BEAR IN THE FOREST

I am deeply grateful to Beatrice Silverman Weinreich, renowned folklorist and editor of *Yiddish Folktales*, for giving me permission to retell "The Bear in the Forest" from her master's thesis, "The Prophet Elijah in Modern Yiddish Folktales." In the early 1920's and 1930's, before the Holocaust, a group of committed young Jewish ethnographers went out into the Jewish communities of Eastern Europe to gather their people's folk and oral traditions. One of the most important of these young Yiddish folklorists was Shmuel Lehman, who did special research on the Elijah tales. Today the YIVO Institute in New York City is carrying on this work by preserving and publishing these stories from the rich heritage of Eastern European Jewry.

THE STRANGE JOURNEY OF
RABBI JOSHUA BEN LEVI

Rabbi Joshua ben Levi is a historical figure who lived during the first century in Lydda in ancient Palestine. He himself was a scholar and spiritual leader renowned for his piety and humility, who came to be associated with Elijah in the lore and legend of succeeding generations. This story is one of the classic tales of Elijah. It can be found in Samuel Segal's book *Elijah: A Study in Jewish Folklore* under the title "Elijah's Ways Are Strange but Just" and in other collections of Jewish folklore, but it was first known to be recorded in a sixteenth-century text by Rabbi Nissim ben Jacob. This story has been incorporated into other religious traditions as well, including the Koran—the holy book of Islam. In the Islamic version, the story is told with the characters of El Khadir, the Wanderer, in place of Elijah, and Musa

(Moses) in place of Rabbi Joshua. The scene where Elijah causes the magical transformation of the stick are unique to my retelling. In the traditional version, Elijah's parting words to Rabbi Joshua end with the admonition, "Do not question the ways of the Creator. For God's ways are just and his eyes are on all men."

WHERE IS ELIJAH?

The short narrative that inspired this story can be found in the book *The Prophet Elijah and the Development of Judaism* by Aharon Wiener. In Chapter V, Wiener recounts a story in which a man goes to a Hasidic rebbe, asking if he will ever see Elijah at his Seder. The rebbe sends the man out to accomplish a task of charity and, at the end of Passover, shows the man his own face in the mirror. A parallel story can be found in Molly Cone's book for children, *Who Knows Ten? Children's Tales of the Ten Commandments*. In all other respects, this story is original.

BIBLIOGRAPHY

Birnbaum, Philip. *The Daily Prayer Book/Siddur Shalem.* New York: Hebrew Publishing Co., 1949.

Bronner, Leah. *The Stories of Elijah and Elisha.* Leiden, the Netherlands: E.J. Brill, 1968.

Elbaz, Andre. *Folktales of the Canadian Sephardim.* Toronto: Fitzhenry and Whiteside, 1982.

Gaer, Joseph. *The Lore of the Old Testament.* Boston: Little, Brown and Co., 1951.

Gaster, Moses. *The Ma'aseh Book,* Vol. II. Philadelphia: The Jewish Publication Society, 1934.

The Holy Scriptures According to the Masoretic Text. Philadelphia: The Jewish Publication Society, 1955.

Ginzberg, Louis. *Legends of the Jews,* Vol. IV. Philadelphia: The Jewish Publication Society, 1934.

Jaffe, Nina. *The Uninvited Guest and Other Jewish Holiday Tales.* New York: Scholastic, 1993.

Jastrow, Marcus. *A Dictionary of the Targunim, the Talamud Babli and Yerushalmi and Midrashic Literature.* Vol. I. New York: Pardes Publishing House, 1950.

Klapholtz, Yisroel. *Stories of the Prophet Elijah*, Vols. I and II. B'nei Brak, Israel: Pe'er HaSefer Publishers, 1978.

Kolatch, Alfred J. *The Complete Dictionary of English and Hebrew First Names.* Middle Village, New York: Jonathan David Publishers, 1984.

Landman, Israel, ed. *The Universal Jewish Encyclopedia: An Authoritative and Popular Presentation of Jews and Judaism Since Earliest Times.* New York: Ktav Publishing House, 1968.

Leach, Maria, ed. *Funk and Wagnall's Standard Dictionary of Folklore, Mythology and Legend.* San Francisco: Harper and Row, 1972.

Lewis, B., Ch. Pellat, and J. Schact, eds. *Encyclopedia of Islam,* Vol. IV. Leiden, the Netherlands: E.J. Brill, 1978.

Patai, Raphael. *The Gates to the Old City: A Book of Jewish Legends.* New York: Avon, 1989.

Piechotka, Maria and Kazimierz. *Wooden Synagogues.* Warsaw: Arkady, 1959.

BIBLIOGRAPHY

Roth, Cecil, ed. *Encylopedia Judaica*. Jerusalem: Keter Publishing House, 1972.

Sabar, Yona. *Folk Literature of the Kurdistani Jews*. New Haven: Yale University Press, 1982.

Sawyer, Ruth. *The Way of the Storyteller*. New York: The Viking Press, 1942.

Schwartz, Howard. *Miriam's Tambourine: Jewish Folktales from Around the World*. New York: Oxford University Press, 1992.

Schwartzbaum, Haim. *Jewish Folklore Between East and West*. Beer Sheva: Ben Gurion University of the Negev Press, 1989.

———. *Studies in Jewish and World Folklore*. Berlin: Walter De Gruyter and Co., 1968.

Segal, Rabbi Samuel. *Elijah: A Study in Jewish Folklore*. New York: Behrman's Jewish Book House, 1935.

Shenhar, Aliza. *Jewish and Israeli Folklore*. New Delhi: South Asian Publishers, 1987.

Silverman, Rabbi Morris. *The Passover Haggadah*. Bridgeport: The Prayer Book Press, 1959.

Weinreich, Beatrice Silverman. "The Prophet Elijah in Modern

Yiddish Folktales." Master's Thesis, Columbia University, New York, 1957.

————.*Yiddish Folktales.* New York: Random House, 1990.

Wiener, Aharon. *The Prophet Elijah in the Development of Judaism: A Depth-Psychological Study.* London: Routledge and Kegan Paul, 1978.

Wineman, David. *Beyond Appearances: Stories from the Kabbalistic Ethical Writings.* Philadelphia: The Jewish Publication Society, 1988.

RECOMMENDED READING

Here are books with other stories about the Prophet Elijah and other Jewish folktales.

Ausubel, Nathan. *A Treasury of Jewish Folklore*. New York: Crown Publishers, 1948, 1975.

Bin Gurion, Micha Joseph. *Mimekor Yisrael: Selected Classical Jewish Folktales*. Bloomington: Indiana University Press, 1990.

Cone, Molly. *Who Knows Ten? Children's Tales of the Ten Commandments*. New York: United Associations of Hebrew Congregations, 1976.

Goldin, Barbara Diamond. *Just Enough Is Plenty*. New York: Viking Children's Books, 1992.

Jaffe, Nina, and Steve Zeitlin. *While Standing on One Foot: Puzzle Stories and Wisdom Tales from the Jewish Tradition*. New York: Henry Holt and Co., 1993.

Nahmad, H.M. *A Portion in Paradise and Other Jewish Folktales*. New York: Schocken Books, 1974.

Noy, Dov. *Folktales of Israel*. Chicago: University of Chicago Press, 1963.

Rush, Barbara. *The Book of Jewish Women's Tales*. Northvale, N.J.: Jason Aronson, 1994.

Sadeh, Pinches. *Jewish Folktales*, trans. Hillel Halkin. New York: Bantam / Doubleday / Dell, 1989.

Schram, Peninnah. *Chosen Tales: Stories Told by Jewish Storytellers*. Northvale, N.J.: Jason Aronson, 1995.

————. *Tales of the Prophet Elijah*. Northvale, N.J.: Jason Aronson, 1991.

Schwartz, Howard. *Elijah's Violin and Other Jewish Fairy Tales*. New York: Harper and Row, 1983.

Singer, Isaac Bashevis. *Elijah the Slave*. New York: Farrar, Strauss and Giroux, 1972.